The Yummiest Githeri

Written and Illustrated by
Kwame Nyong'o

A very special thanks to Aarti wa Njoroge, Janet Omega, Mama and Baba Juno, Simon Kariuki and Tavia Nyong'o for all their help with this book.

Wanja skipped her way to school through her home town in beautiful central Kenya. The area around her town is always so green and fertile, the farmers there grow lots of different crops.

Mum had packed Wanja her favourite dish for lunch, *githeri*. *Githeri* is made from maize, beans and other yummy vegetables.

Oftentimes in school Wanja would think about lunch and the *githeri* she was going to eat. She dreamed of *githeri* in maths class....

...and even during english class.

"Riiing, riiing!" went the bell and Wanja rushed outside to take her meal. But as she popped open her lunch box, two girls sneaked up behind her.

"Ha ha! Look at you, you're just eating *githeri* from home! Us, we get to buy chips…and hot dogs!" Shiko laughed at Wanja.

"*Githeri* is so *shao!*" went Anita. The girls then ran off giggling, leaving Wanja sad and confused.

As Wanja walked home that day she thought to herself "*Githeri* must not be as nice as chips and hot dogs. I'll ask Mum if she can give me money so I can also buy them for lunch."

"*Sema* Wanja, how was school today?" greeted Mum.

"*Poa*...but Mum, some girls at school get to buy chips and hotdogs for lunch. Can I have those too instead of *githeri*?"

"Now Wanja, *githeri* is good for you. Just imagine all the sun and rain that helps our food grow. *Githeri* is healthy, full of vitamins and minerals because of all the goodness it gets from nature."

Wanja's eyes brightened up a little. "Really?"

"Yes, just keep eating your *githeri* and you'll see that you'll keep getting stronger and smarter," reassured Mum.

"Oh, okay," Wanja mumbled.

The next day at school when Wanja was just about to eat her *githeri,* guess who showed up?

"Ha, ha, ha!" snickered Shiko and Anita. "There's the village girl again eating her village food! Look what we have today, chips, hot dogs and even...
...soda! *Woi*!"

Wanja rose up. "You know what? I really like *githeri*. It's very, very yummy and it gives me lots of energy! You should try some."

"Yeah, whatever," mocked the girls eating and sipping on their sodas noisily.

Later that afternoon, it was Wanja who got the answers correct in class…

…and later during sports, it was Wanja who ran extra fast!

The next day at lunchtime, Shiko and Anita tip-toed up to Wanja and asked softly, "Can we… try some of your…*githeri*?"

Wanja looked at them in surprise. "Oh, well…sure you may", and passed them her dish.

The girls each tried some, their curious chews turning into delighted gulps.

"Mum is going to be cooking more *githeri* this weekend. Why don't you all come over and help?" Wanja asked the girls. "It's going to be fun, even my cousin is coming."

"Sounds good!" said Shiko and Anita eagerly.

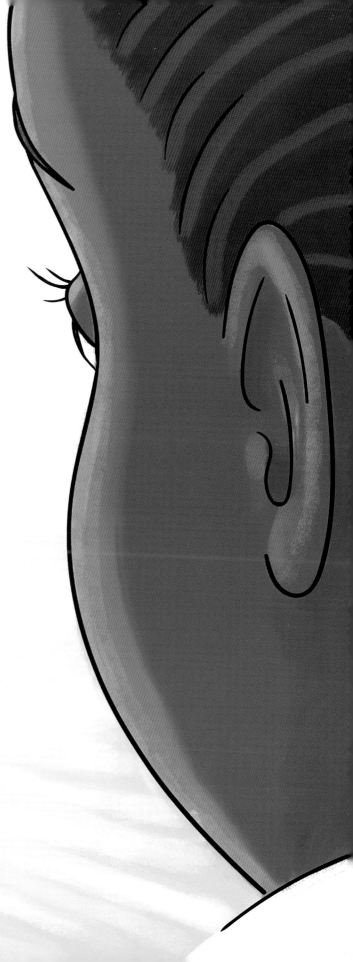

That Saturday there was a big *githeri* making party at Wanja's house.

"Chop, chop, chop," could be heard as Mum cut up onions and tomatoes.

"Zzz, Zzzz, Zzz," went the peeler over the carrots as cousin Wanzilu skinned them.

"Tsh, tsh, tsh," was the sound as Wanja, Shiko and Anita shelled fresh beans.

"Here's the *sufuria* to cook the *githeri* in!" smiled Mum as she grabbed a large pot.

"Mum, can I help *asha* the stove?" asked Wanja pointing to the charcoal cooker.

"Sure you may, my dear," said Mum. "We must boil the maize and beans on it for a long time until they are fully cooked."

"Why do maize and beans take so long to cook?" wondered Wanzilu.

"Because maize and beans are actually seeds and are quite tough, that's why they need more time to cook and soften," Mum explained.

"Really? We never knew!" exclaimed the girls.

"'Now you know," winked Mum.

The girls played games until the maize and beans were ready.

Mum heated up some *ghee* in another *sufuria*. She used it to fry in the onions, garlic, carrots and tomatoes. She then mixed in the maize and beans, *dhania* and salt, stirring well so that all the ingredients would cook together evenly.

"Smells so good!" the girls cheered.

After a few minutes the delicious meal was ready and Mum served everyone the yummiest *githeri* that they had ever, ever had.

The next week at school, Shiko and Anita called out to Wanja. "Hey Wanja, can we join you for lunch?"

"Yes, of course," said Wanja.

"Guess what we have today?"

Wanja thought to herself, "Hmm, maybe could it be…?"

Map of Kenya

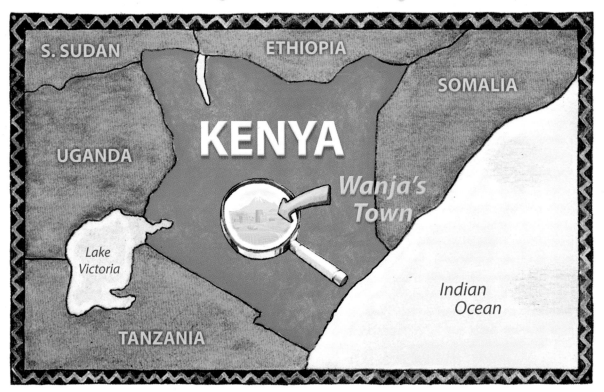

Swahili to English Dictionary

Asha: To turn on

Dhania: Coriander

Ghee: A traditional clarified butter

Githeri: A traditional maize and bean stew from central Kenya

Maindi: White maize

Poa: Cool, I'm fine

Sema: Speak, tell me

Shao: (slang) From the village

Sufuria: A metal cooking pot

Woi: (slang) A term of laughing at or mocking someone